Market Day

CAROL FOSKETT CORDSEN
illustrated — by — DOUGLAS B. JONES

Dutton Children's Books

*For farmers' market days with Dick, Ellie,
Nancy, and Susan. For yellow house days with Gail,
Gaines, Chris, and Caroline. And, as always,
for every day with Ben.*

C.F.C.

For Zeke and Chelsea

D.B.J.

DUTTON CHILDREN'S BOOKS
A division of Penguin Young Readers Group
Published by the Penguin Group
Penguin Group (USA) Inc., 375 Hudson Street, New York, New York 10014, U.S.A.
Penguin Group (Canada), 90 Eglington Avenue East, Suite 700, Toronto, Ontario M4P 2Y3, Canada
(a division of Pearson Penguin Canada Inc.)
Penguin Books Ltd, 80 Strand, London WC2R 0RL, England
Penguin Ireland, 25 St Stephen's Green, Dublin 2, Ireland
(a division of Penguin Books Ltd)
Penguin Group (Australia), 250 Camberwell Road, Camberwell, Victoria 3124, Australia
(a division of Pearson Australia Group Pty Ltd)
Penguin Books India Pvt Ltd, 11 Community Centre, Panchsheel Park, New Delhi—110 017, India
Penguin Group (NZ), 67 Apollo Drive, Rosedale, North Shore 0632, New Zealand
(a division of Pearson New Zealand Ltd)
Penguin Books (South Africa) (Pty) Ltd, 24 Sturdee Avenue, Rosebank, Johannesburg 2196, South Africa
Penguin Books Ltd, Registered Offices: 80 Strand, London WC2R 0RL, England

LIBRARY OF CONGRESS CATALOGING-IN-PUBLICATION DATA
Cordsen, Carol Foskett.
Market day / by Carol Foskett Cordsen ; illustrated by Douglas B.
Jones.—1st ed.   p. cm.
Summary: The Benson family is so busy preparing for their day at a farmers' market that
they not only forget to feed the cow, they leave the farmyard gate open and the hungry cow
follows them, making a mess of the market.
ISBN 978-0-525-47883-6
[1. Farmers' markets—Fiction. 2. Cows—Fiction. 3. Farm produce—Fiction.
4. Stories in rhyme.] I. Jones, Douglas B., ill. II. Title.
PZ8.3.C8167Mar 2008   [E]—dc22   2007028489

Published in the United States by Dutton Children's Books,
a division of Penguin Young Readers Group
345 Hudson Street, New York, New York 10014
www.penguin.com/youngreaders
Designed by Sara Reynolds
Manufactured in China • First Edition
1 3 5 7 9 10 8 6 4 2

*H*arvest sun up. Over bay.
Over farmhouse. Start of day.

Family farm cow still asleep.

Farmhouse family dreaming deep.

Farm cow waking. Tardy MOO!

Bensons rising. Much to do.

Bread and butter. Apple jam.
Hats on. Shoes on. Screen door slams.

Passing farmyard. Passing cow.
Cannot stop to feed her now.

Lugging ladder out of shed.

Picking apples. Green. And red.
Apple boxes, in a stack.
Filling farm truck front to back.

Finally finished. Loud "Hurray!"
Bensons set for Market Day.
Zipping. Zooming. Running late.

No one closing farmyard gate.
No one looking back behind.
Market Day on all four minds.

Tents and tables. Driving slow.
One spot open. End of row.
Busy Bensons. All four out.
Not aware of stares and shouts.

Not aware of market trouble
coming closer, on the double.

Mr. Spencer catches pies.
Mrs. Spencer wipes her eyes.

Matthew's yellow onions sail.
Out of buckets. Out of pails.

Sacks of Jewel's potatoes spill.

Nathan's pumpkins roll downhill.

Busy Bensons. Apples out.
Not aware of stares and shouts.
Not aware of market trouble
coming closer, on the double.

Gracie glances. Sees a flutter.
Pea pods fly. And Gracie mutters.

Tumbling cans of fishing bait.
Clayton glances up too late.

Braided ropes of garlic flip.
Crates of Kyle's tomatoes slip.

Dolls Irene made. Teddy bears.
Tumble out of tree-trunk chairs.

Ryan and Marie MEOW.
Hide beside a rusty plow.

Farmer Gilbert's table wiggles.
Baby Edith jiggles. Giggles.
Ears of sweet corn. Twist and drop.
Upside down on tasseled top.

Busy Bensons. Looking out.
Well aware of stares and shouts.
Well aware of market trouble
coming closer, on the double.

Hungry farm cow. Hungry MOO!

Bensons know just what to do.
One green apple. One more. Red.
Benson farm cow finally fed.

Bensons help with Market mess.
Market open. Big success.

Benson family. Home asleep.

Benson farm cow dreaming deep.

Harvest moon up. Over bay.
Over farmhouse. End of day.